TINY LANE BOOKS

Leo Goes
Ice Skating

TINY LANE BOOKS

www.tinylanebooks.com

ISBN: 9798422041824

For orders and information please visit
www.tinylanebooks.com

This book is dedicated to my two beautiful children. They make every day as lovely and as magical for me as the first time skating on the ice is for Leo in the story.

They have shown me how wonderfully full of love life can be and I hope that my books bring a little joy to your family too.

Leo sat with his mama and asked her
the same question he asked every day.

'Mama, when will I be big enough?'

He longed to be like his big sister Thallie and go to school...

ride a bike...

and go ice skating.

'Don't hurry little one,
your time will come,'
his mama would say.

But today, when he asked his question, her reply was different.

She smiled and said, 'today little Leo, you are ready to go ice skating.'

Leo was excited. He imagined himself gliding on the ice like a graceful penguin.

But then he felt worried.

How would he balance?
Would he slip over?
Would anybody hold his hand?

His lower lip trembled.

His mama could see that he felt nervous.

So she picked him up and told him, 'don't worry little Leo, we will show you how.'

Leo's big sister showed him how to put on his boots.

The laces were tricky and the boots didn't feel like his normal shoes.

He wobbled on the ice.
It certainly felt strange.

His mama and Thallie
held him so tightly.

Thallie whispered to him,
'don't worry Leo, I will look after you.'

But the ice was cold and Leo started to shake.

Just as he was about to give up, he heard a familiar voice.

His daddy!

'Look up Leo, I'll be here to catch you.'

Leo's smile was the biggest you've ever seen and he bravely took his first tiny solo steps on the ice.

His sister danced around so gracefully in circles and Leo giggled.

'Well done, Leo' she shouted from across the ice!

'You're doing so well!'

He felt so happy and he wasn't scared anymore.

He held his mama and daddy's hands and sailed around the rink.

He felt like he was flying.

Leo imagined he was a perfect, elegant white swan on a frosty lake, gliding smoothly along.

And then a little cheery red robin, tip toeing delicately on a frozen stream.

Leo's mama and daddy watched him joyfully as he pretended to be in a marching band, spinning and jumping and twirling a baton.

He felt like an aeroplane about to take flight.
Speeding along the runway and then soaring high,
sailing through the clouds.

He wondered if this was how the birds
felt who floated across the sky?

So free and so light!

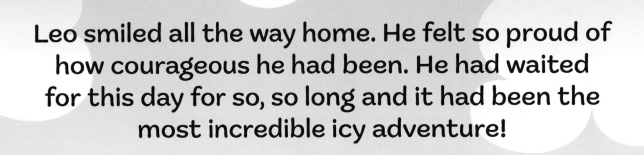

Leo smiled all the way home. He felt so proud of how courageous he had been. He had waited for this day for so, so long and it had been the most incredible icy adventure!

Later that night as his mama tucked him into bed, she kissed his forehead and told him how brave he had been to skate on the ice for the very first time.

Leo smiled sleepily, he felt so warm and cosy.

As his weary eyes closed, he whispered, 'can we do it again tomorrow mama?'

'Of course,' she said. 'Sweet dreams little Leo, I love you my sleepy head.'

THE
END

Activity:

1. Who helped Leo to put on his ice skates?

2. How do you think Leo felt the first time he stepped onto the ice?

3. Can you name one animal Leo imagined he was?

4. How do you think Leo felt on the way home?

5. What did Leo ask his mama just before he went to sleep?

Printed in Great Britain
by Amazon

16319861R00018